D0204796

No Arm in Left Field

NO ARM IN LEFT FIELD

by Matt Christopher

Illustrated by Byron Goto

Little, Brown and Company
BOSTON NEW YORK TORONTO LONDON

Library of Congress Cataloging-in-Publication Data
Christopher, Matthew F
No arm in left field.

[1. Baseball—Stories] I. Goto, Byron, illus.
II. Title.
PZ7.C458No [Fic] 73-12296
ISBN 0-316-13964-5
ISBN 0-316-13990-4 (pbk.)

HC: 10 9 8 7 6 5
PB: 10 9

VB

Published simultaneously in Canada
by Little, Brown & Company (Canada) Limited

Printed in the United States of America

to Kenny VanSickle

No Arm in Left Field

1

TERRY DELANEY took a couple of steps closer to Mick Jordan to make sure his throw wouldn't fall short, and winged the ball. The worn, dirt-stained sphere arced through the air and landed in Mick's outstretched glove. A short throw didn't bother him, but he just didn't have the arm for throwing a long distance.

"Who'd you play with on Long Island?" Mick asked, pushing his long black hair out of his eyes.

"The Fall City Tigers." Terry smiled.

"Know where we finished up? Next to last!"

Mick laughed. Terry had been telling him about the small town on Long Island where he had lived before moving to Forest Lake, a suburb in eastern Pennsylvania. Terry's father, an engineer, had taken a job with a mining concern and brought his family here in the middle of the winter. Within weeks Mrs. Delaney had joined the Great Books Club in Forest Lake, and Connie, Terry's fifteen-year-old sister, had become a varsity cheerleader. The family settled easily into the life of their new town.

Terry, himself a junior high student, had liked winter sports but was pleased that at last summer had finally rolled around, for with it had come his favorite sport, baseball.

"You have a league here?" he asked.

"Of course," said Mick, reaching forward to grab Terry's soft throw. "I play with the Forest Lakers. We're having practice in a little while. Want to come with me?"

Terry's eyes brightened. "You don't have to ask me twice!" he replied happily.

Just then a voice shouted from across the street. "Hey, Mick!"

Mick held up his throw, turned, and looked at the kid who had yelled. Terry looked, too. A tall, dark-haired boy wearing a knit sweater and bell-bottom pants came running across the street. He stopped on the sidewalk, let his gaze linger a while on Terry, then motioned to Mick.

"Come here, will ya?" he said.

His voice was commanding. Terry felt

a sudden change in the atmosphere, as if it had become charged with electricity.

Mick tossed the ball to Terry. "Just a second, Terry," he said, and trotted over to the newcomer.

"Who's the Negro kid?" Terry heard the newcomer ask plainly.

Terry's face grew hot, but his eyes narrowed and he stared at the boy. He didn't hear Mick's response, nor could he hear anymore of what the newcomer said. He had a good idea of the gist of it, however, and that was enough. He shook his head and looked away.

After a minute Mick's voice was loud enough for Terry to hear. "Come on. He's okay, I tell you."

Terry looked at them, and noticed that the newcomer had a baseball glove and was wearing sneakers.

Terry turned and started for his house, tossing the baseball into the air and catching it as it came down. He wasn't going to wait around all day. He whistled in order to drown out the voices behind him.

It had happened again, he thought, his stomach churning. *A white kid who doesn't like a black kid. But I bet that one of his favorite baseball players, or football players, is black.*

"Hey, Terry! Wait a minute!"

He paused without turning around, and heard Mick's footsteps pounding up behind him.

"Terry." Mick stopped before him, breathing hard. "Terry, I'm sorry."

Terry smiled. "Oh, that's okay. I've seen his kind before. He on your team?"

"He's our shortstop."

"Is he good?"

"Yes, he is."

Terry looked over his shoulder, saw the kid begin to walk briskly away and then pause near a bush to look back.

"He's waiting for you," Terry said. "Better get going."

"Aren't you coming?" Mick asked.

"No." Terry flashed a grin. "Go on, Mick. Don't worry about me. I'll be all right."

Mick shook his head. "I don't know what to say, Terry. I wanted him to meet you. I was surprised when he said he — he didn't want to." He wiped his forehead with the back of his hand. "I feel funny, Terry."

Terry chuckled. "I know. That's because it's brand new to you. Not to me, though I'll never get used to it. Go ahead,

he's waiting. I've got things to do, anyway." He turned and headed for the porch.

"See you later, Terry," Mick said.

"Sure, Mick."

Terry opened the screen door and stepped onto the porch. He closed it and saw Mick running across the lawn toward the kid who was waiting for him. He wasn't sure, but he thought he saw the kid smile.

Connie met him as he stepped into the house. Even though she was three years older she was only an inch taller than her athletic brother.

"Who's the kid with Mick?" she asked.

"I don't know. Mick didn't tell me and I didn't ask him."

"Where are they going?"

"To the ball field. Their team's practicing."

He started past her and she grabbed his arm. Her eyes were hard as she looked at him. "I know you want to play, Terry. Why didn't you go with Mick?"

He reached over and gently lifted her hand from his arm. "Because I'm black, my dear sister, and that other kid just don't like black." A smile cracked his face. "You've heard of *that* before, haven't you?"

Connie didn't flinch. "Maybe that kid's the only one who feels that way. There are other black families in this town."

"I know. But that kid is sure to have friends, and his friends are likely to go along with him. You should've heard him. 'Who's the "Negro" kid?' he asked Mick in that tone they use and loud enough so I can hear. Right away I pegged him. He's a leader, Connie. He's the type guys follow."

"You're just guessing, Terry. You don't know for sure."

"Okay, I don't know for sure. But I'll bet on it."

The sun was dropping toward the western horizon when a knock sounded on the door. Mrs. Delaney answered it.

"Terry, it's Mick," she said.

Terry left the TV set where he had been watching a sports program and met Mick at the door. Mick's hair was tousled and his face shiny with sweat.

"Hi, Terry," he greeted him. "Got some news for you. We need an outfielder."

Terry crossed his arms. "Don't look at me," he said.

"But you said that you'd like to play!" Mick exclaimed. "And there's nobody else. Come on, Terry. Please come to our next practice. I've told Coach Harper about you."

Soft footsteps sounded behind Terry and he looked over his shoulder. The warm, pleasant face of his father grinned at him.

"Hi, Mick," Mr. Delaney said. "I heard what you said to Terry. I think it's a good idea."

"What about that kid who was here earlier?"

"Tony Casterline? He can lump it for all I care!"

Terry laughed. Still, he wasn't sure he

wanted to join a team on which even one member had a grudge against a black boy's playing. And, as he had said to Connie, there could be others.

He finally agreed, however, when Dad, Mom and Connie put in their nickel's worth. He would give it a try, at least. Who knew but what his playing – if he could only perform well – might make Tony Casterline forget his prejudice and turn him into a friend? Such things happened. If only his arm were stronger . . .

The next afternoon Mick stopped at the house. Together they walked to the ballfield where Terry was introduced to Coach Don Harper and the members of the Forest Lakers baseball team. Some nodded their greeting, some shook hands. Tony Casterline was one of the former.

Terry couldn't help but feel conspicuous. He was the only black boy in the group. He noticed, though, that there was another boy whose skin was darker than the others, whose features suggested a nationality from, he guessed, a country in South America. The boy's name was Caesar Valquez.

Terry wondered briefly how Caesar was accepted when he had first come to Forest Lake. Or was he born here?

"Okay, guys," Coach Harper said, carrying a bat and ball to the plate. "Outfielders, hustle out there. Terry, get out in left. Infielders, play catch."

Coach Harper's hits to the outfielders ranged from line drives to sky-reaching blows. Terry didn't have a miss and welcomed the coach's praises of "Nice going,

Terry!" and "Hey, we've got an outfielder!"

Batting practice turned into a lot of fun, too. The team batted twice around and Terry knocked his share of grounders and long flies to his usual corner, deep left. His bunting, though, suffered.

"We're having a practice game with the Boilers tomorrow afternoon," the coach said to Terry when practice was over. "Like to have you here."

Terry smiled. "I'll be here," he promised.

He almost forgot Tony Casterline's coldness as he walked home with Mick. All he could think about was telling Mom, Dad and Connie that the coach liked his playing and wanted him at the practice game tomorrow.

Then he remembered something else,

and he turned to his friend. "Thanks, Mick," he said. "If it weren't for you, I wouldn't be playing baseball."

Mick's eyes glimmered. "Aw, forget it, Terry," he said. "Somebody would've asked you to play."

A hot June sun blazed down on the baseball field the next afternoon. The teams tossed a coin to see who would bat last, and the Boilers won. Pitching for them was a red-headed left-hander, Lefty Wallace.

The first three batters for the Forest Lakers were Jeff Roberts, Tony Casterline and Terry Delaney. Terry couldn't believe it. Third batter!

Lefty's speed worked like magic. Both Jeff and Tony popped up to the infield. After fouling two pitches Terry struck out on a high, outside throw.

3
24

"That was over your head, man!" Tony cried.

Terry ignored him as he dropped the bat, got his glove, and ran out to his position.

The first pitch Mick Jordan delivered to the Boilers' lead-off man was hit through the hole between first and second base. The man held up at first as right fielder Caesar Valquez fielded the ball and pegged it to second.

The second batter failed on two bunt attempts, then drilled a long fly to deep left. Terry backpedaled for it, caught it, then whipped it to third base. The ball barely reached the halfway point between him and the infield. The runner on first – after tagging up – ran to second, then bolted to third.

Third baseman Ed Caliel rushed out

to receive the throw in, but the runner was safely on base by the time he got it and turned to throw.

"Hold it!" Mick yelled.

A second voice sliced through the air, and Terry's ears filled with its terrible ring.

"Hey! See that? Terry hasn't got an arm! He can't throw worth beans!"

2

TERRY TWINGED. He couldn't rid himself of his poor throwing arm. It was his big weakness.

Once, a couple of years ago, he had played second base, where he didn't have to throw very hard. But his coach had discovered that Terry was better at catching flies than grounders, and so had transferred him to the outfield. Terry liked that better and had played there ever since, even if he did have trouble when a long fly was hit while men were on base.

He saw the angry look on Tony's face,

and heard a chuckle come from center fielder Rich Muldoon.

"Why don't you trade in that arm, Terry?" the tall, skinny kid hollered at him. "You sure can't get a worse one!"

Terry grinned. "I'll make up for it in other ways, Rich!" he yelled back.

With one out, Mick pitched to the next batter. The Boiler smashed a hot, sizzling liner directly at Ed Caliel at third. The runner on third started toward home, then stopped. He slipped as he tried to get back to third, and Ed doubled him up. Three outs.

"Nice play, Ed," Terry said as he trotted up beside the stocky third baseman.

Ed glanced at him, nodded, and looked away.

"Muldoon, Philips, Caliel," Coach Harper announced. "Get on, Rich."

Rich put on his protective helmet, stepped to the plate, took his swings and struck out. Bud Philips hit a high bouncer to the pitcher for the second out and Ed grounded out to short.

Mick held the Boilers hitless. Then, in the top of the third, Stu Henderson drilled Lefty Wallace's second pitch through the pitcher's mound, forcing Lefty to dance a momentary jig. It was the Forest Lakers' first hit of the game and the guys got excited.

Caesar Valquez stepped to the plate, dug his sneakers into the soft dirt as if he were going to wallop one of Lefty's pitches into no man's land, and then stuck the bat out for a bunt.

Foul.

Caesar stepped out of the box, glanced

at the coach and stepped back in again. Another bunt, and again a foul.

"Hit away, Ceez!" Coach Harper yelled.

Caesar blasted the next pitch to center for an easy out. Mick, last man in the batting order, removed the metal doughnut from the fat part of his bat, plodded to the plate, dug his sneakers firmly into the dirt, and watched the first pitch breeze by him.

"Strike!" yelled the ump.

"Clout it, Mick!" Terry cried.

The pitch, and Mick swung. A hot grounder to second base! The Boiler second baseman caught the hop, snapped it to second for the first out, the shortstop whipped it to first. A double play.

The Boiler fans roared as the teams exchanged sides.

Bottom of the third. *Hope nobody*

knocks one too deep in left, Terry thought as he ran out to his position. *I don't want Tony Casterline to be able to embarrass me again.*

A high pop fly to Stu accounted for the first out and Terry breathed a sigh of relief. Then Mick drilled a pitch over the heart of the plate and the Boiler batter drilled it back at him like a rifle shot. It knocked Mick's glove off and bounced out to center for a hit.

Man on first and one out.

Mick toed the rubber and threw. *Crack!* A hefty clout to deep left. Terry turned and bolted back toward the fence, then looked over his shoulder, lifted his glove and snared the ball – a spectacular, one-handed catch. He stopped in his tracks and pegged the ball in to Tony Casterline, throwing it as hard as he could. The ball dropped short, as he expected, and he saw the Boiler runner beeline to second.

"Old no arm!" Tony yelled as he ran out to get the throw in. The runner held up at second.

Terry's heart pounded. Not only from running, but because of Tony's sarcastic remark. Old no arm! That darn guy didn't even give him credit for the catch!

A shot over short scored the Boilers' first run. Terry ran up, caught the ball on a bounce and pegged it successfully to Jeff Roberts at second. The hitter held up on first. Coming in closer to Tony, Terry was able to see a scowl on the shortstop's face.

The Forest Lakers settled down. Stu, crouched behind home plate in his catcher's gear, tried to liven up the team with his peppery chatter. Although this was just a practice game, the guys were serious about every play. Terry wondered how much more serious they could be when league play actually started.

Mick worked the next Boiler batter to two balls and two strikes, then fanned him with a curve.

Jeff, leading off for the Lakers in the top of the fourth, struck out. Tony then laced a pitch through short for a single. Terry came up, hoping to redeem himself for his first strikeout. Lefty threw two inside pitches, then fired one high and outside, which Terry liked.

He swung – and missed. Another high, outside pitch. Again he swung – and missed.

"Two . . . two!" the ump bellowed.

Terry stepped out of the box, rubbed

the bat firmly around its skinny handle, then stepped in again and lambasted Lefty's next pitch to left center field. Tony raced around to third and Terry held up on second for a clean double. Standing on the bag Terry noticed Tony looking at him appraisingly.

The handful of Forest Laker fans cheered Terry, and he felt pleased. He had put himself and Tony in scoring position. Now it was up to the next batters.

Rich Muldoon didn't help. His pop-up to third made it two outs. It was up to Bud Philips. Bud, a lanky, light-haired, left-handed batter, strode to the plate in that lazy fashion of his and watched the first pitch sail by him as if he were watching a parade. He didn't look as if he were going to swing at the next pitch either until after the ball had left Lefty's hand and was halfway to the plate.

Crack! A bullet drive to right center, and both Tony and Terry scored! Ed grounded out to end the rally. Forest Lakers 2, Boilers 1.

The change in the lead seemed to have affected the Boilers. They weren't able to get a man on first base in their half of the inning. In the fifth Stu, Caesar and Mick went down one, two, three. So did the Boilers.

Jeff, leading off for the Lakers in the top of the sixth, singled on the first pitch and scampered to second base on Tony's scratch single. Terry, hoping to knock in at least one run, swung hard at a high, outside one – and missed. He let a low pitch slide by for strike two, then swung hard again at another one he liked – high and outside.

"Strike three!" cried the ump.

"Oh, come on!" Tony yelled angrily. "Somebody knock us in!"

Nobody did.

"This is it!" Coach Harper said as the Lakers ran out to the field. "Let's play heads-up out there!"

Mick worked hard on the Boiler lead-off man and struck him out on the 3–2 pitch. The infielders snapped the ball around the horn, then returned it to Mick.

Mick took his time, then threw one low and inside. Bat met ball and Terry sprinted forward as he saw it heading for short left field. He reached low for the shallow drive and caught the ball near his sneaker laces. He was within ten feet of Tony when he slowed up and tossed the ball to the shortstop.

"Nice catch," Tony said, and smiled crookedly. "Too bad nobody was on second. You might've thrown him out – seeing you didn't have far to throw."

"Guess I was lucky," Terry said as he turned and trotted back to his position. He tried not to get sore. Maybe one of these days – soon, he hoped – Tony would realize that Terry could catch, run and hit well enough to make up for his poor arm, and stop his sarcastic remarks.

Mick walked the next Boiler, the next batter popped out to Ed, and that was it. The Forest Lakers won, 2 to 1.

"Nice game, Terry," Mick said as they stood by the water fountain, waiting for their chance to get a drink.

"Thanks, Mick," Terry said, wiping his sweating brow. "You, too."

A couple of strange guys came up and looked at Terry. They were about his age and wore baseball caps.

"Nice hit you got, Delaney," one of them wearing glasses said. "Bet you won't get to first base on us."

A chuckle rippled from him as he nudged his partner and walked away.

"Who are they?" Terry asked curiously.

"Jim Burling and Dave Wilson," said Tony, who was standing nearby. "They're the battery for the Yellow Jackets, the team we play our first league game with. They've got your number, Terry. You're a sucker for high, outside pitches."

3

FELLAS," Coach Harper said. "Before you leave I've got some nice news for you. There's a movie on the Oakland-Cincinnati World Series tomorrow night at the Forest Lake Hotel, sponsored by the Forest Lake Lions Club, and all of us are invited to attend. How about that?"

A chorus of satisfied shouts resounded from the boys. Terry was especially pleased for the opportunity. He hadn't seen any of the World Series games on television.

Suddenly he remembered that tomorrow night his father had planned to take the family out to dinner. The conflict bothered him. He liked to go out for dinner, but he wanted to see the World Series movie, too.

"Fine," the coach said. "The movie will be shown at seven-thirty. I'll have someone telephone each of you and arrange to pick you up."

"Are you going, Terry?" Mick asked.

"I'd like to," Terry replied. "But we've planned to go out for dinner."

"Skip the dinner," Mick suggested, smiling. "You can't always see a World Series movie."

Terry shrugged. "Okay. I'm sure my dad will take us out for dinner again sometime!"

Terry saw a scornful look come over Tony's face. *Can you beat that?* he thought. *He even resents my going to see a World Series movie with the team!*

Their eyes locked. Then Tony looked away, tapped a couple of his friends on their shoulders, and walked off with them.

"Ready to go?" Terry asked Mick, hoping nobody could hear his pounding heart.

Mick glanced at the three boys leaving. "Let's wait a minute," he said.

"Why? For Tony and those guys to get way ahead of us?" Terry grinned. "If I don't mind them, why should you?"

Mick's eyebrows pulled together above the bridge of his nose. "You mean it doesn't bother you, the way he looked at you and all that"

"I've met guys like Tony before, Mick," Terry said. "I'll always keep meeting guys like him. My father says that'll be something I'll have to live with the rest of my life, and as far as I can see I'm not the one with a problem. Tony is."

"But doesn't it *hurt?*"

"Sure it hurts. But not as much as it used to." He chuckled. "At least, he hasn't called me any dirty names yet – and if he knows what's good for him, he better not."

Mick laughed and socked Terry lightly on the shoulder. "Come on," he said, and they started off the field. "You know, Terry, I can't see why any guy – black or white – can't like you. You know what I'd probably do if I were in your place?"

"What?" Terry asked.

"I'd, well, I'd . . ."

Mick looked at Terry, a vacant expression in his eyes.

"You'd what, Mick?"

Mick inhaled deeply, then breathed out a sigh. "Darn it, Terry, I don't know what I'd do," he admitted.

They walked the rest of the way home in silence, and when Terry told his parents that he wanted to go to the World Series movie instead of to dinner with them, his father didn't blame him.

"We can all have dinner together anytime," he said. "But a World Series movie isn't shown very often."

The next evening the Delaneys left at 6:30, with Terry waiting in the living room for the telephone call. Twice he almost dozed off. The clock on the mantle said 7:00, then 7:15, then 7:30. Still the phone didn't ring.

Had he been forgotten? He tried phoning Mick, but no one answered.

7:45 . . . 8:00 . . .

Suddenly the phone rang. Terry leaped out of the chair and grabbed the receiver. "Yes?" he said excitedly.

"Hello. This is Mrs. Williams of the Great Books Club," said a warm, soothing voice. "Is Mrs. Delaney there?"

Terry's heart sank. "No, she isn't," he answered politely. "Can I take a message?"

"No," the woman said. "I'll call again tomorrow. Thank you."

The phone clicked. Terry hung up and went back to the chair, dejected. He should have gone to the dinner, he thought, instead of sitting here like a bump on a log.

He picked up a magazine and was reading it when his parents and Connie returned from dinner. They stared surprisedly at him.

"What happened?" his father asked. "Was the movie canceled?"

"Nobody called," Terry said cheerlessly.

"I'm so sorry," Mrs. Delaney said. "I guess you should have come with us after all."

He went back to his reading, and was only half concentrating on the story when the phone rang again. Quickly he dropped the magazine and went to answer it.

"Hello?"

"Terry, this is Mick."

"Yes, Mick?"

"Too bad you missed the World Series movie. It was great!"

Terry's hand froze on the receiver. He

stared at the clock on the wall. Ten after nine!

"Nobody called me," he said huskily.

"Didn't Tony call you?"

"*Tony?* Was *he* supposed to call me?"

"Yes! He told me you weren't going. He said that you decided to go to dinner with your family!"

"The liar!" Terry cried. "He never called me at all!"

"The rat," Mick said softly.

Terry saw Tony the next day at practice. He was boiling mad. "Tony, I heard that you were supposed to call me last night," he said, trying to control his rage.

Tony blushed. "I thought you were going to dinner with your family," he said.

"I didn't say I was," Terry shot back. "I said that we had *planned* to go, but that I would go to the World Series movie instead. You must have heard me."

Tony's lips pressed together, then spread apart in a forced smile. "You didn't miss anything," he said. "It wasn't that good."

"I *bet* it wasn't," Terry snapped, and stamped angrily toward the pile of bats. He selected one he liked, slipped a metal doughnut over the fat part of it and began swinging it hard back and forth over his shoulder.

4

LATER, WHILE waiting for supper, Terry and Mick played catch on the front lawn. Terry was trying to strengthen his throwing arm. He *had* to be able to peg the ball to second or third base when it was hit to deep left. Mick had put a handkerchief in his glove to cushion the throws and was catching them with hardly a wince.

"How am I doing?" Terry asked.

"I don't know," Mick answered. "It's hard to tell. Let's go to the ballfield after supper."

Mick's father came by and paused on the sidewalk.

"Hi, Mr. Jordan," Terry greeted him. "I'm trying to build up my throwing arm."

"Hi, Dad," Mick said.

"Hi, boys," Mr. Jordan greeted them. He was tall, yellow-haired, and had the long, lithe build of an athlete. "Mind a bit of advice, Terry?"

Terry held up his throw and looked at Mr. Jordan. "Anything you want to tell me is sure welcome, Mr. Jordan," he replied honestly.

Mr. Jordan grinned. "Well, it isn't much, but it might save you a lot of torture later on." He slapped at an annoying bee. "I understand what you're trying to do, but at your age you'd better not throw too hard nor too long or you might come up with a permanent injury in that arm.

You're just a kid yet. Your arm isn't strong enough to take it."

"That's why I'm throwing harder," Terry explained, frowning. "So it will be stronger."

"You're taking a chance, Terry," Mr. Jordan warned. "A big chance." He shrugged and started toward home. "Well, don't say I didn't warn you."

Terry smiled. "I won't, Mr. Jordan," he promised, "because, as of right now, I'm going to take your advice."

Terry waited for Mr. Jordan to walk on, then looked at his friend. "Now there's a guy who turns me on, Mick," he said happily. "Not even my own father tells me things like that."

He pegged the ball to Mick, then heard footsteps on the porch behind him.

"That's because your own father doesn't

know a thing about baseball," said a voice. Terry turned to see his tall, broad-shouldered father standing behind the screen door, a genial smile on his lips.

Terry chuckled. "Did you hear what Mr. Jordan told me, Dad?"

"I sure did," Mr. Delaney said. "And I think that it makes a lot of sense."

He came off the porch, stopped beside Mick, and began to play catch with the boys.

Presently a dune buggy with a huge flower painted on its hood came buzzing up the street, crept up to the curb, and stopped. Out of it hopped Tony Casterline and Jeff Roberts. Terry saw that the driver looked to be about nineteen or twenty, wore long hair, and had a striking resemblance to Tony.

The two boys waved to him as he stepped on the gas and sped away.

Terry looked at Tony and Jeff without speaking. His first impression was that they had come to see him, since the dune buggy had stopped directly in front of his house. But the guys motioned to Mick and ignored him completely.

"Excuse me, Mr. Delaney," Mick said, and ran over to them.

Terry smiled at his father. *Don't worry, Dad,* his look said. *Those guys don't impress me a bit.*

They continued to play catch – just the two of them – and were interrupted when Mrs. Delaney came to the door and told her husband that he had a phone call. He excused himself and went into the house.

A minute later Tony and Jeff started to leave, and Mick returned to his post to continue playing catch with Terry.

"Hey, you guys," Terry suddenly called to them. "If you want to join us one of you can use my glove. I've got another one in the house, and one guy can sit out for a while."

Tony and Jeff looked at him, said something to each other, then returned to the lawn. Terry smiled and sent his glove spinning toward the boys.

"You use it," Tony said to Jeff.

Jeff caught it and put it on. As Terry started toward the house for his other glove, Tony called to him, "Never mind, Terry. I don't think your glove is going to feel right to either of us."

Terry looked at him; the real meaning

behind Tony's statement hit him like a baseball bat. What Tony meant was that he wouldn't use Terry's glove just because it was Terry's.

Before Terry could decide what to say, Jeff took off the glove and tossed it back to him. "Here," he said. "I really don't think it fits, either."

Terry's face felt hot. He had hoped that his friendly gesture would bear fruit, that it might start to close the gap between them. But his offer had been turned against him in order to humiliate him. His eyes blazed. "All right. If the glove isn't right, let's play bare-handed. That okay with you guys?"

Jeff gazed in sheepish inquiry at Tony. "Yeah, that's okay."

Tony shrugged.

Terry winged the ball to Tony who

gasped at the ball's impact on his hands. "Take it easy, will you, Terry?" Tony asked.

Terry, seeing Tony's discomfort, smiled a bit and nodded agreement. They lobbed the ball between the four of them.

"Your father ever play professional baseball?" Tony asked as he caught a soft throw from Mick.

"No. Just sandlot," Terry replied.

"My father played in the majors," Tony said, a spark of pride in his voice.

"He did? With whom?"

"The Minnesota Twins."

Terry's heart skipped a beat. He had never before met a kid whose father played major league baseball.

"He was an infielder," Tony added.

They tossed the ball back and forth a few more times, and Terry could see that neither Tony nor Jeff were enjoying catching it bare-handed. After awhile Tony said that they had to leave, and they did.

"Aren't you going to ask me what they wanted?" Mick asked.

Terry shrugged. "I figure you'd tell me if you wanted to," he said.

Mick smiled. "They told me that our first league game is Tuesday against the Yellow Jackets. But I already knew that. I think it was just an excuse for them to stop here and cause a bit of trouble."

Terry nodded. "I figured that," he said. "And I'm glad they did. I guess maybe next time they might *want* to use my glove."

Mick chuckled. "I guess they will," he said.

5

THE YELLOW JACKETS had a picture of a fat bee on the front left side of their jerseys. They had first raps and looked extremely confident of winning their first game.

On the mound for the Forest Lakers was Woody Davis, a slim kid with arms like spindles but with plenty of speed. A crowd was divided between a large group in the stands behind the backstop screen and a smattering in the small bleachers behind first and third bases. It was a hot June day and a lot of the women were fanning themselves to keep cool.

The Yellow Jackets' lead-off hitter looked for a walk, and almost got it as Woody worked the count on him to 3–2. Then Woody slid a pitch by him.

"Strike three!" yelled the ump.

In left field Terry Delaney wished that if a ball were hit out to him it would be a shallow drive, one that he wouldn't have trouble throwing in to the infield. The thought had hardly left his mind when *bang!* – a long hit zoomed out to deep left! He ran back . . . back . . . lifted his glove and caught the fly over his head!

The Forest Laker fans cheered as he pegged the ball in. They didn't know, though, how hard his heart was pounding and how relieved he was.

A pop fly to the infield ended the top half of the inning.

Jeff Roberts, leading off for the Forest

Lakers, put on his protective helmet, stepped to the mound, and faced the Yellow Jackets' short, husky pitcher, Jim Durling. Ready to follow him were Tony, Terry, and Rich Muldoon.

Jim released a couple of high pitches, then grooved one down the middle. He grooved the next one too, and Jeff smashed it to center field for a single.

Tony got the signal from Coach Harper to bunt, and laid one down neatly just inside the third-base line. The Yellow Jacket third baseman, waiting for exactly this to happen, nevertheless didn't play in close enough to field the bunt and get Jeff at second. He managed, however, to throw Tony out at first.

Terry let an inside pitch go by for a strike, then swung at a high, outside one that he missed for strike two.

“Bring ’em down, Terry!” yelled Tony, who had run back to the bench.

Terry stepped out of the box and rubbed his hands in the soft dirt, while a chorus of yells rose from the fans. He returned to the box. In came a pitch he liked, and he swung. Foul ball!

Nothing and two. He felt nervous and sweaty. Hundreds of pairs of eyes were focused on him, waiting to see what he would do.

A wide pitch. One and two.

Another pitch looked good to him. He swung hard – and missed. “Strike three!” the ump yelled.

“That was a mile high, Terry!” Tony shouted. “You’ve got to bring ’em down, man!”

Terry tossed the bat aside and re-

turned, head bowed, to the bench, the roar of the fans lingering in his ears.

"That was high and outside, Terry," Coach Harper said evenly. "Next time step a few inches closer to the plate. See what happens."

Terry nodded.

Rich, the Forest Lakers' cleanup hitter, belted a foul ball into the third-base bleachers, then lambasted a high pitch to deep center. The ball was caught and that was it for the Lakers' half of the inning.

The Yellow Jackets' lead-off hitter cracked Woody's first pitch to right field for a neat single, then made it to second on a sacrifice bunt. First baseman Bud Philips brought the ball to Woody after the put-out, talked to him a minute, then returned to his position.

Woody threw two wide pitches to the

next Yellow Jacket, then grooved one. *Crack!* A blow to deep left center! Both Terry and Rich bolted after it. Terry reached it first, picked it up and heaved it to second base.

The ball hit the ground far short of the bag. Second baseman Jeff Roberts snorted disgustedly as he ran after it. The runner on second scored. And the hitter, after rounding first and second bases, made a beeline for third. Jeff, grabbing up the ball on the outfield grass, pegged it quickly to Ed Caliel. The throw was high and the runner slid safely into the bag.

"A triple!" Tony grunted, casting a burning look at Terry. "A good arm would've got him at second!"

Terry, hurt by Tony's stinging public accusation, bent over, cropped a handful of grass and tossed it angrily aside. Most of the time he was able to laugh off remarks guys made about his poor throwing arm. But it was getting so that Tony's remarks always hurt.

My throwing arm is just an excuse, Terry told himself. *It's my color that Tony doesn't like.*

The Forest Lakers settled down and Woody Davis faced the next batter. There was one out and a man on third.

The pitch. Then a smashing blow to second! Jeff fielded the ball and whipped it to first. The runner on third started for home, then dashed back.

The next batter drove a sizzling line drive over Woody's head, scoring a run. A strikeout ended the Yellow Jackets' romp. Yellow Jackets 2, Forest Lakers 0.

"Get on, Bud," Coach Harper said.

Bud did. He singled to left and Ed

Caliel scored him on a triple to right center. Stu Henderson popped out and Caesar Valquez grounded out, bringing up Woody Davis. The fans cheered the young pitcher as he took the metal doughnut off the fat end of his bat and stepped to the plate. He windmilled the bat a couple of times, then stood still as he waited for the pitch. It came in and he belted it for a single over third, scoring Ed. Jeff flied out, ending the second inning.

Terry ran out to left, wondering how long he'd last if he muffed another play. Bob Decker was a utility infielder and outfielder, and Mick Jordan was able to handle an outfield position if necessary. Either one could take his place if Coach Don Harper saw fit to take him out.

Woody fanned the first Yellow Jacket, then grooved the first pitch to the next batter. The blow was a long high drive to left that made Terry get on his bicycle. He made a leaping catch that drew applause from the crowd – including some Yellow Jacket fans – and pegged the ball in to Ed. It bounced and rolled most of the way to the third baseman, but it didn't matter. No one was on base.

Jeff missed a hot drive. Then a safe hit to left field, which Terry caught on the first hop, left men on first and third. A good arm might have thrown the runner out at third, but Terry's weak throw gave him time to make it standing up.

The runners perished on base, though, as Woody struck out the next batter. Greatly relieved, Terry ran in from the outfield.

Tony led off in the bottom of the third, smashing out a double to start things rolling. Terry stepped up to the plate, then moved a few inches closer to it as Coach Harper had suggested. He waited for a pitch he liked, hoping desperately to knock Tony in, and struck out on the same pitch that had become his bugaboo – the high outsider.

"I guess that standing closer to the plate doesn't help," observed the coach. "You've just got to learn to bring 'em down, Terry. Jim Burling's got good control, and he knows your weakness."

"I've been trying," Terry confessed.

"I know." The coach patted him on the knee. "Take it easy the rest of the game. I'll have Bob Decker take your place."

"Okay," said Terry. Deep inside he was relieved by the coach's decision.

He watched Rich hit a double, scoring Tony. Then Bud singled, scoring Rich.

Those were the only runs the Lakers were able to run up that half inning. They were in front now, 4–2.

The fourth inning went by scoreless. The Yellow Jackets picked up a run in the fifth, but neither team scored again and the Lakers won, 4–3.

The guys rushed at Woody, yelling and cheering their first victory. Terry found himself among them, forgetting everything that had happened on the field, thinking only about this wonderful moment. He flung his arms around the guys and cheered with them.

Not until he felt his arm being lifted away from a shoulder did the spell break. The shoulder belonged to Tony Casterline, and the look was plain enough: *Keep your arm off me.*

6

TERRY STARTED in the game against the Roadrunners, a fiery team that wore all-white uniforms except for the picture of a roadrunner on the front of their jerseys. It was Thursday, the first of July, and the temperature was soaring in the nineties.

The Forest Lakers had first raps and Mick Jordan was scheduled to pitch. On the mound for the Roadrunners was a left-hander, Hank Rhodes.

The game got underway and Jeff Roberts, leading off, took a 1–2 count, then blasted a pitch directly at the center fielder. One out. Tony grounded out on the first pitch and Terry stepped to the plate.

Swoosh! A swing and a miss.

"Too high, Terry!" Tony shouted.

Terry grimaced. *I wish Tony would keep his mouth shut while I'm batting,* he thought angrily.

"Ball!" High and outside.

"That' a way to look, Terry!" Mick said.

Swoosh! Another swing and a miss.

"Oh, no!" Tony moaned. "He did it again!"

Terry stepped out of the box, leaned over and ran his hands up and down the smooth sides of the bat. Then he stepped in again, braced his feet and held his bat high and off his shoulder.

The pitch. It came in belt-high. Terry

stepped into it and swung. *Crack!* A bullet-piercing drive to deep left! The ball kept going . . . going . . . going . . .

Over the fence! A home run!

Terry dropped his bat and circled the bases, the cries of the fans ringing warmly in his ears. Nothing had sounded so great in a long, long time.

He was met at the plate by each player, who shook his hand as he ran by. Even Tony was there to meet him, saying, "Nice blast, Terry."

Rich flied out, ending the top of the inning.

Mick had trouble with the first Road-runner and walked him on four straight pitches. A bunt sent the man down to second, then a line drive over second scored him. 1–1.

In the top of the second, Bud Philips

singled, Ed flied out, and Stu Henderson hit into a double play.

In the bottom of the second Mick again had trouble with his control. He walked the first man up, then redeemed himself by catching a pop fly when the next batter tried to bunt.

A drive between first and third allowed the runner to reach third base. Then, with men on first and third, the next batter delivered a solid blow to deep left that again made Terry get on his bicycle. The ball dropped over his head for a hit. He ran after it as it bounced to the fence, picked it up and heaved it as hard as he could toward the infield.

Ed Caliel, as he should have, played close to his third-base sack. Tony came out to the outfield to receive Terry's throw in, but not far enough. By the time he got

the ball and pegged it home, both runners had scored — *and so had the hitter.*

It was a home run. The Roadrunner fans went wild.

Terry stood glued to the spot from where he had pegged the ball, looking on with his legs spread-eagled. *Darn you, Tony,* he thought. *That would not have been a home run if you had come closer. You could've thrown him out!*

He didn't know how they got the next hitters out, but they did.

"I'm sorry, Mick," Terry said as he ran in and reached the pitcher's side. "That was my fault."

"Your fault, my eye," Mick said. "Tony knows you've got a poor arm. He should've run out farther for your throw."

Terry agreed, but said nothing.

The Forest Lakers soon picked up two

runs, beginning with a single by Caesar Valquez, then successive hits by Jeff, Tony and Terry. Terry had doubled, giving him a two-for-two hitting record in the game so far.

Mick held the Roadrunners hitless in the bottom of the third, and Lefty Rhodes did the same with the Forest Lakers.

It was in the bottom of the fourth that the Roadrunners started to lambaste Mick again, getting two hits right off the bat. Then Mick walked two men, forcing in a run. He had three balls and no strikes on the next batter when Stu called time, ran out to the mound and talked to Mick.

The talk hardly helped. Mick fired a strike, then grooved the next pitch too, only to see it go for a hit over short. Two runs scored and Coach Harper called time. He took Mick out and called in the reserve pitcher, Woody Davis, who had been warming up behind the third-base bleachers.

Woody pulled the Lakers through without giving up a hit, and managed to pitch the rest of the game with no Roadrunner scoring. The bats of the Lakers weren't sounding off loud enough, however, and the Roadrunners took the game, 7–3.

Terry had been up four times: knocking a homer, a double, walking once and striking out his last time up. It was the strikeout Tony Casterline remembered, for it was the last out of the game.

"You just can't get it into your head, Terry," he said with biting sarcasm. "You struck at two pitches that were way high and outside. You could've walked and saved Rich a chance to bat. We had two men on. And Rich was due to hit."

Terry looked at him. His eyes shone like hard glass. "And you could've come out farther on that hit that went up against the fence to save a run," he countered. "Why didn't you?"

Tony's face reddened. He looked around, saw Jeff, and went toward him. Mick grinned at Terry.

"That's telling him," he said.

Terry saw his father come running toward him and the boys. Behind him were Mrs. Delaney and Connie.

"Tony! Jeff!" Mr. Delaney yelled. "Lose or not, you're all invited to our place for ice cream and cake!" he said cheerfully.

Terry looked happily at his father and mother. No one could say that Dad wasn't trying to keep harmony among the boys.

"I . . . I'm sorry," Tony stammered. "I've got someplace else to go."

"Oh, that's too bad," said Mr. Delaney. "Maybe next time."

"I'll be there, Mr. Delaney," Rich Muldoon said.

"So will I," said Ed Caliel.

A similar chorus rose from the other guys, including Coach Harper, whose blue eyes twinkled. "Me, too, Mr. Delaney," he said.

"Mark," Mr. Delaney said.

Coach Harper grinned. "Mark," he echoed. "And I'm Don."

They shook hands, smiled at each other, and Mr. Delaney said, "Everybody come right over. All we have to do is put the stuff on the table."

Some of the players rode to Terry's house with Coach Harper. But most of them, including Terry and his family, walked.

There wasn't enough room for every Laker to sit at the red picnic table, so Mr. Delaney brought out a card table and chairs. Mrs. Delaney and Connie served the refreshments.

Terry looked at the group, pleased as he could be that most of the members of the team had accepted his father's invitation. Only Tony and Jeff weren't there. He wasn't surprised that Jeff hadn't come. Tony had probably influenced him not to.

A noisy vehicle came buzzing down the street, and Terry saw Harry Casterline's dune buggy pulling up to the curb. He was alone.

For a moment he sat there, the motor idling. He was gazing at the group, and Terry surmised that he was looking for Tony.

"Come in, Harry!" Mr. Delaney yelled.

"Join us for some ice cream and cake!"

Harry Casterline seemed to hesitate a while, as if considering the invitation. Then he shut off the motor and came striding across the lawn, looking sharp in a black sweater and flashy, bell-bottom pants.

"Where's Tony?" he asked curiously.

"He said he couldn't come," Mr. Delaney replied. "Wait. I'll get you a chair."

"Thanks, Mr. Delaney," Harry said. "I can stand."

His smile faded slightly as his thoughts seemed to stray – stray, Terry thought, to his brother Tony.

7

AFTER THE ice cream, cake and soft drinks were finished, Coach Harper and the members of the Forest Lakers thanked the Delaneys for the treat and left. Harry Casterline thanked them too, then turned to Terry.

"Would you like to ride in a dune buggy, Terry?" he asked.

Terry's eyes widened. "You bet I would!"

"Do you mind, Mr. Delaney?"

The big man's eyes shone as he looked from Harry to his son. "Not at all."

"Thanks, Dad!" cried Terry. "Oh – can Mick come along?"

"Why not?" Harry waved to Mr. Delaney and headed for the dune buggy. "See you, Mr. Delaney! Come on, guys!"

Terry and Mick raced across the lawn to the little vehicle. Mick climbed up behind the seat and grabbed hold of the metal guard bar. "You sit in front, Terry," he said, his face glowing with excitement.

Terry sat down in the passenger seat and buckled on his seat belt. Harry slid in behind the wheel, buckled on his seat belt, then started the motor and drove off with a roar from the twin exhausts.

"Tony say why he couldn't go to your party?" Harry asked.

"No," Terry replied. "He just said he had someplace else to go."

The dune buggy sped smoothly down

the street, turned left at the intersection and went up a steep grade.

"How are you and Tony getting along, Terry?" Harry asked.

Terry was surprised at the question. "Okay, I guess," he said half-heartedly.

"You're being modest," Harry said. "I know better. That kid brother of mine was brainwashed about black people by our parents a long time ago, and it's going to take some doing to change him. I just hope you two guys will become friends. I'd like Tony to realize that the color of a person's skin has nothing to do with what he believes in and how he lives."

"Any reason why your parents don't like black people, Harry?" Terry asked freely.

"Yes and no, Terry," Harry replied. "My parents never knew a black family.

All they knew was what they read in the papers or heard what white people said. Then my father was beaten out of a job as a construction foreman by a black guy. My father admits that the better man won, but it didn't help him see blacks as great guys. I don't know. It's a pretty complicated thing to talk about. I confess that I was like my folks until I was old enough to get away from home more and meet a lot of people, both white and black. I don't choose my friends by their race anymore."

"I wish Tony was like that," Terry said. "We'd have a real good baseball team if he was."

Harry laughed. "Yes, I suppose you would. I've seen how he plays his position when a ball is hit to you. Oh, he'll come around to seeing things differently someday. I'm sure of it."

"I hope so," Terry said, but he thought, *I don't know. I've heard that song before.*

They reached the outskirts of Forest Lake, crossed an abandoned railroad track, and started past a dirt road when Mick shouted, "Hey, Harry! Motorcycle Hill is to our left! Ever climb it?"

"With this dune buggy?" Harry smiled.

"Yeah!" said Mick, a mischievous grin spreading over his face.

"No. But we can try it." Harry looked at Terry. "Okay with you, Terry? Motorcycle Hill is pretty steep. It's where cycle nuts try their luck. Some make it, some don't."

Terry shrugged. He couldn't say no. He and Mick were Harry's guests. Whatever

Harry wanted to do was all right with him.

"Okay by me," he said.

"Fine," said Harry. "It's been something I've wanted to do with this dunie bug ever since I got her."

He pulled into a driveway, backed out and returned to the dirt road. He sped over it, gravel banging up against the fenders, till they reached a high, barren hill several hundred yards to their right. He geared down the motor and turned onto the wide road that led to the hill. The slope was about two hundred feet high and gouged from where hundreds of angry motorcycle wheels had struggled to climb to its top.

"Still game?" Harry asked.

"It's your dunie bug," Terry replied.

Harry shifted gears and started for the hill. When they reached it, the nose of the dune buggy rose as the little four-wheeler began to climb. Up, up it went, the motor roaring, the wheels spinning, kicking back dirt and gravel.

Laughter shrilled from behind Terry, and he turned to see Mick hanging onto the guard bar, his hair flying in the wind.

"Go, buggy, go!" Mick shouted gleefully.

They reached the halfway point and were still climbing. The dune buggy bounced, slid sideways, bucked like a bronco. Higher and higher it climbed, while Mick's laughter rang louder and louder. The hill got steeper. Terry felt an excitement mixed with an equal dose of fear.

He had trust in Harry Casterline, though. He was sure that nothing could happen.

But something did.

The dune buggy struck a rock that jolted its front end. The wheels twisted to the right, jerking the steering wheel out of Harry's hands. Horror-stricken, Terry felt the vehicle begin to careen over.

"Mick, jump out!" Harry shouted. "Terry, unbuckle your seat belt and jump!"

Fingers trembling, Terry unbuckled his seat belt and jumped.

8

TERRY STRUCK the ground, fell to his knees, got up, and scrambled out of the way of the overturning dune buggy. The vehicle missed him by a foot as it rolled over.

On the other side, safely out of its way, were Mick and Harry, watching the dune buggy start to roll down the steep hill. Each time the guard bar hit, the vehicle bounced high into the air, spun halfway around, struck the ground with its wheels, then bounced again.

They watched in shocked silence until

the dune buggy stopped rolling at the bottom of the hill. It shuddered and lay on its side like a dead animal.

Harry and the boys scrambled down to it. Its two free wheels were still turning.

"Boys," Harry said sadly, "I'm sorry. I – I'm just glad that both of you got out of it safely."

"I'm glad that you did, too," Terry said, still trembling.

Harry walked round to the side of the vehicle, lifted it a little, and looked at the boys. "Think we can do it?" he said.

"We can try," Mick answered.

The three of them, with Harry in the middle, combined their strength to lift the vehicle and gradually succeeded in getting it right-side up.

"We did it!" Mick exclaimed triumphantly.

"Well," Harry observed, breathing a tired sigh, "the key's still in it."

He hopped in and turned the key. *Whir! whir!* The motor burst to life. "Well, guys, that much is okay," he said. "Hop on!"

The boys hopped on, and Harry put the dune buggy in gear, stepped on the gas, and turned the wheel. "Oh, oh," he said. "The steering wheel's damaged."

With some effort he made the turn, however, and drove to the main road that led into town. There was a *bumpety-bump* in the ride that hadn't been there before, just as there were dents in the fenders and hood that weren't there be-fore.

They drew amused glances from pedes-trians and drivers on their way, and even-tually pulled into a garage. Harry talked to a mechanic, then said to the boys, "Well it's the hospital for the dunie bug for the next week or two. My house is a couple of blocks away. Let's clean up, then I'll drive you home in my father's car."

At the house Terry met Tony and Tony's mother and father. All three of them looked wide-eyed with astonishment as Harry explained what had happened. Terry sensed the hostility in Mr. Casterline's eyes, and remembered what Harry had said about his parents. All they knew about black people was what they had read and heard, he'd said. Terry felt that he was being scrutinized as he returned from the bathroom.

"Well, you look better," Mr. Casterline said, smiling. "You didn't get hurt?"

"No."

"Not even a scratch?"

"No. I was lucky."

"How about you, Mick"

Mick grinned. "Just got dirty when we hopped off the dune buggy," he said, cheerfully.

"You were all lucky," Mr. Casterline admitted.

Terry hoped that the man would talk more to him; that talking would start him to realize that he was a human being first and black second, just as he himself was a human being first and white second.

Terry remembered what Tony had said about his father's having played in the big leagues, and suddenly he felt happy because, for the first time in his life, he was in the presence of a former big league baseball player.

Maybe if I said something about his

major league career he would talk a little more and forget some of those prejudices he's had against black people, Terry thought. Harry had gone into the bathroom to wash up and would be out in a minute.

Terry's heart pounded, and he forced a smile. "Mr. Casterline, I heard that you used to play in the big leagues," he said. He paused, still overwhelmed by the thought of it. Mr. Casterline was a big man – at least six foot three – and probably had knocked a lot of home runs.

A curious look entered the big man's eyes. "Who told you that?" he asked.

"Tony," Terry said.

Mr. Casterline frowned and stared at his son. "When did I ever tell you that, Tony?" he inquired.

Tony blushed. "Well, you were with

the Minnesota Twins, weren't you?" he said.

"No. I was with their farm team," Mr. Casterline replied emphatically.

"What's the difference?" Tony turned and headed for the outside door, but not before Terry had seen the color of his ears. They were pure red.

"Come back here," Mr. Casterline ordered.

Tony came back. His father's eyes were hard as he gazed at him. "There's a lot of difference," he said sharply. "You shouldn't have said that. You gave Terry the wrong impression." He smiled at Terry. "No, I never played in the big leagues, Terry. I was close, but never close enough."

9

THE FOREST LAKERS played the Thunderheads on Tuesday, July 6, with the Lakers having last raps. The day was cloudy, and radio reports indicated that there was a forty percent possibility of rain.

Mick Jordan, on the mound for the Forest Lakers, kept the Thunderheads hitless during the top of the first inning. The Lakers did better. Jeff led off with a walk, going to third on a double by Tony, which put the home team in excellent scoring position.

Terry stepped into the box and watched Ted Joseph, the tall pitcher for the Thunderheads, turn and squeeze the ball as if he were trying to squash it. Ted wore thick glasses, threw with a side-arm delivery, and had good control.

"Strike!" yelled the ump as the first pitch grooved the plate.

Another pitch, high and outside. The kind Terry liked. He swung – and missed. "Strike two!"

"Get 'em down, Terry!" Tony yelled from second base.

Terry stepped nervously out of the box, leaned over and rubbed his sweating hands in the dust. *Why couldn't he powder those high, outside pitches?* he wondered. *Why did they always look easy to hit?*

He brushed the dust off his hands,

grabbed the bat and returned to the box. Two men on. A good opportunity to score a couple of runs and make Tony back off his high horse.

Ted Joseph breezed in the pitch. Terry watched it anxiously. It looked good. He swung.

"Strike three!" shouted the ump.

"Oh, no!" Tony's voice boomed from second.

Head bowed, Terry returned to the dugout. He dropped his bat and sat down, shaking his head.

"You still go after those high, outside pitches, Terry," Coach Harper said. "Ted Joseph knows it, and he's got pretty good control."

"I guess I'm a real sucker for 'em," Terry admitted.

Mick, sitting beside him, socked him

gently on the knee. "Don't worry, Terry. One of these days you'll get that pitch out of your system and knock that ball all over the lot."

Terry grinned. "Oh, sure. And be another Hank Aaron. Right?"

Crack! Terry looked up and saw Rich Muldoon high-tailing it for first base. Then he saw the ball arcing toward left center field. A roar broke from the Forest Lakers' fans as Jeff Roberts crossed the plate, Tony Casterline at his heels.

Terry clapped and tried to avoid Tony's eyes as the shortstop trotted in to the dugout behind Jeff.

"Coach," Tony said, breathing hard, "did you tell Terry that he's still swinging at those high, outside pitches?"

"I reminded him," Coach said. "And he

knows it. Quit harping on it. You're not the coach here, you know."

Terry's eyes locked with Tony's. He couldn't mistake the frigid look that told him more than a hundred words.

He remembered the day at Tony's house when he had asked Mr. Casterline about his major league baseball career, and Mr. Casterline said that he had never been in the majors. He remembered the look Tony had given him then – a look mixed with embarrassment and resentment. Tony, Terry felt sure, wouldn't forget that moment for a long time to come.

Bud Philips smacked a clothesline drive directly at the third baseman, who stepped on the bag before Rich could tag up. A double play. Three outs.

Cheers exploded from the Thunderhead fans as the teams exchanged sides.

Mick lowered the boom on the first batter. The next socked a low pitch to left center for a neat double. Mick then walked two men in succession to fill the bases, and Stu called time.

The catcher trotted to the mound to talk to Mick. So did Jeff, Bud and Ed. Tony remained at deep short. Terry thought that he had never seen Tony act this way before. Tony was usually one of the first to run in to the pitcher, to help him settle down, to tell him that the situation wasn't as dark as it seemed.

This time, for some reason, Tony was staying out of it. Did the coach's remark have something to do with it? Terry wondered.

The guys returned to their positions.

The ump called time in, and the game resumed.

Crack! A single to right! A run scored. The second runner tried to score too, but a hard throw from Jeff to Stu, after Caesar Valquez had pegged the ball in from the outfield, threw out the runner. A pop fly to Ed Caliel ended the threatening rally.

Ted Joseph's side-arm delivery worked effectively during the bottom half of the second inning, holding the Lakers scoreless. Then the Thunderheads threatened again. This time their bats thundered loudly and produced results.

Two consecutive hits to deep left had Terry scrambling madly for the ball and pegging it to third. Both times the ball had dropped far too short and two runs scored easily. Both times Ed Caliel had run out to get the ball and relay it home.

But his throws had fallen short, too. It would have taken a mighty arm to throw out a runner from where Ed had thrown it.

"Old no arm!" Tony Casterline yelled at Terry. "When are you going to trade it in?"

"Why don't you come in for the relay?" Terry shouted back. "Maybe we can throw out some of those runners at third!"

"Oh, sure!" Tony replied.

But wasn't that reasonable? Terry thought. *If Tony ran out and intercepted the throw in, Ed could cover third base. Even if the relay to him was too late to nab the runner at third, at least it would hold him on base, or get him out at home if he dared to risk running there.*

Mick fanned a Thunderhead, but that only seemed to increase their rage. Their booming bats knocked in two more runs.

"Tony!" Terry yelled. "Call time! Talk to Mick! Maybe he's too tired to keep pitchin'!"

Almost at once Tony lifted a hand and cried, "Time, ump!" The base umpire lifted his arms as a signal to the plate umpire, who lifted his arms too and called for time. The infielders ran in and huddled around Mick, and Terry's heart warmed a little. It was the first time that Tony had ever heeded his suggestion.

Then Woody Davis walked to the mound and Mick walked off. A cheer from the Forest Lakers' fans burst out for Mick, who kept his gaze glued unhappily to the ground all the way to the dugout.

There were two men on as Woody threw in a half a dozen warm-up pitches. Then time in was called and Woody went to work. He had trouble with his control and walked the first man, filling the bases. He took his time on the next hitter, and struck him out. Two outs.

The stands were silent as the next Thunderhead came to the plate. There was even silence in the infield, until Terry cried, "Come on, you guys! Get alive! Say something!"

Ed started the chatter. Tony joined in. Presently all nine men were shouting in a chorus of voices filled with spirit and enthusiasm.

The pitch. *Smack!* A sky-reaching fly to short left center field. Terry ran after it, shouting, "I've got it! I've got it!"

He heard another voice yelling too. "I'll take it!"

He was positive, though, that he had

a better chance to catch the ball, since he was running toward it. He reached for it. Just as he caught it someone collided into him and down they both went.

When he regained his senses he saw he had run into Tony.

10

"THAT WAS MY ball, Terry. I yelled for it," Tony said hotly as he sat on the ground, glaring.

"I yelled for it, too," Terry countered, rising and straightening his cap.

Tony got up slowly, and Terry wondered if he was hurt.

"I was under the ball, waiting for it, when you plowed into me," Tony went on, still fuming.

There was a shout from center fielder Rich Muldoon, and Terry realized that the teams were exchanging sides. He ignored Tony and ran off the field.

Coach Harper was standing in front of the dugout, waiting for him and Tony.

"You guys all right?" he asked, concerned.

They nodded.

"That was my ball," Tony insisted, going past the coach to the dugout. "I was waiting for it."

"He's right, Terry," Coach Harper agreed. "That *was* his ball. Didn't you hear him yell for it?"

"Yes. But I . . . Well, I was sure it was mine, too. That's why *I* yelled."

"He was waiting for it," the coach pointed out, "while you were still running. Better watch it the next time. A collision might turn out worse."

"Yes, sir," Terry promised.

"And you, Ed," the coach turned to the third baseman, "should've yelled, too. It's your job as well to let the guys know who should catch that ball."

Ed Caliel looked sheepishly at him. "I wasn't sure," he said apologetically.

"Make sure," the coach said. "Yell someone's name, even if it's just to prevent a collision. Tony and Terry were lucky that neither one of them was hurt. Okay. Let's play ball. Who's the first batter?"

"I am," Jeff Roberts said.

The wiry second baseman already had on his protective helmet. He stepped to the plate, waited out Ted Joseph's pitches, and got his second free pass to first.

The Forest Lakers' bench was like a funeral wake. Not a sound came from it even when Jeff trotted to first base. The Thunderheads' lead of 5 to 2 seemed to have muzzled the Lakers' enthusiasm.

Terry reflected on the fly ball he had gone after and the collision with Tony. He realized he had jumped from the skillet into the fire. He had given Tony another excuse to taunt him.

He saw Tony step to the plate, and remembered he was up next. He put on a helmet, selected his favorite bat, and stood beside the dugout.

Tony flied out.

Terry walked to the plate, let a pitch go by for ball one, then swung at one of those high, outside ones he liked so much. *Swish!*

"Oh, come on, Terry," came Tony's disgruntled remark.

Then *crack!* A hard blow between third

and short. Terry bolted to first and Jeff advanced to second.

Rich grounded out, however, and Bud popped to first to end the threat.

The Lakers held the Thunderheads scoreless in the top of the fourth, then rallied in the bottom half of the inning. A single by Ed, and then a triple by Caesar Valquez scored the Lakers' third run of the game. Woody's single drove in Caesar, making the score Thunderheads 5, Forest Lakers 4.

Again in the fifth inning the Thunderheads weren't able to get a man on. The Lakers came up, and Rich's long clout over the left field fence tied up the score.

With the score tied, excitement began to mount. In the sixth, Woody grooved a pitch down the center of the plate. *Boom!* The ball sailed out like a rocket to left center field. Terry chased after it, caught it on the first hop and pegged it to Rich, who relayed it to second base. The runner started past the bag, then spun and slid back to it as second baseman Jeff Roberts caught the ball and put it on him.

"Safe!" yelled the base umpire.

Jeff argued the call for a moment, then gave up and tossed the ball to Woody. Terry grinned. Jeff was a fireball when he disagreed on a decision.

A ground ball to third. Ed fielded it nicely and whipped it to first. One out.

A big right-hander stepped to the plate. Terry backpedaled a few steps. *Crack!* A hard blow to left! Terry started to run back toward the left field foul line. The ball hit in fair territory and bounced to the fence. Terry sprinted after it, picked it up and pegged it in to Ed who had run out for the throw. Ed then fired it to Tony, who was covering third, and Tony tagged the runner.

"Out!" boomed the ump.

But a run had scored. The Thunderheads were back in the lead, 6–5.

They couldn't score again and the Lakers went to bat with their backs against the wall. Caesar flied out to short. Then Woody chalked up his second hit of the game, a double. Jeff swung hard at two pitches in an effort to drive in the tying run, but grounded out to third. Tony tried hard too, and managed to draw a walk. With two on and two outs, Terry strode to the plate.

"Belt it, Terry!" Mick yelled. "Just a single's all we need!"

Terry grounded out.

11

THE FOREST LAKERS lost their next two games – to the Cornhuskers and the Boilers – and were in the doldrums.

"Chin up," Coach Harper said encouragingly. "It's not the end of the world."

For Terry it was close to it. There was a parallel between him and the team, he figured. Both were losers. There was a chance for the Lakers to start winning, but would there be for him?

Tony Casterline was still hostile toward him. The gap in their relationship hadn't closed a bit. As a matter of fact, it seemed to have widened.

On Monday, July 19, Terry and Mick were walking to the game with the Yellow Jackets when Mick mentioned something that Terry wished he hadn't.

"Did you get invited to Tony's birthday party?" he asked

Terry stared at him. "You must be kidding."

Mick laughed. "I'm sorry. He still doesn't like you, does he?"

"Not a bit," Terry said. "Sometimes I think the situation between us is worse than the first time we met."

"His father speaks to you, doesn't he?"

"He says 'Hello' when he sees me. A couple of times he even paid me a compliment. He isn't all thawed out, though. I can tell."

"Harry's all right, though, isn't he?"

"Oh, yes. Harry's okay." Terry remembered the day that Harry Casterline had driven him and Mick up Motorcycle Hill. "His dune buggy fixed yet?"

Mick nodded. "Saw him with it yesterday."

The game started with the Yellow Jackets taking first raps. Woody Davis was on the mound for the Lakers. It was a clear, warm day and the bleachers were packed.

Nothing happened in the first inning. The Yellow Jackets threatened to score in the top of the second as their lead-off hitter lambasted a long triple, but third base was as far as he got.

The Forest Lakers broke the scoreless tie in the bottom half of the second inning when Ed came through with a surprising triple and scored on Stu Henderson's scratch single to short. Then, in the top of the third, the Yellow Jackets' bats began singing a tune that meant disaster to the Lakers. Two runs scored on back-to-back doubles. A third run scored after a hit to short left field which Terry caught on the first hop and whipped in to home in an effort to nab the runner.

The Yellow Jacket beat the throw by two steps. Terry was certain that anyone else could have thrown the man out easily. He turned unhappily and went back to his spot, waiting to hear a disparaging remark from Tony. Surprisingly, it didn't come.

A pop fly, a strikeout, and a fly to Terry ended the bad half inning.

Tony singled to start off the bottom half of the third, and Terry got the signal to bunt. He waited for the pitch, stuck out his bat and *crack!* A pop-up to the pitcher!

Tony had started to second and was sprinting back to tag up when the pitcher whipped the ball to first.

"Out!" cried the ump.

Terry stood in the batter's box, staring at Tony as he came trotting in to the dugout. Their eyes locked.

"You call that a bunt?" Tony snorted.

"I didn't say it was," Terry replied calmly.

Terry followed Tony to the dugout.

"You shouldn't have run, Tony," Coach Harper said firmly. "On a bunt you wait until the ball is on the ground. You should know that."

"Sorry," Tony muttered as he squeezed in between Caesar and Woody. Mick pushed aside to make room for Terry.

"It was my fault, too," Terry said as he sat down. "A horse could've bunted better than that."

Rick doubled to left center. Bud's fly to right ended the inning.

Nothing significant happened in the fourth. The infield seemed as quiet as a cemetery and Terry tried to put some spark into it. "Come on, guys! Talk it up! Chatter!"

They came to life. They chattered. Their voices joined together, became one. Ed smiled at Terry. "That-a-boy, Terry," he said. "That's what we needed."

Woody walked the first man in the fifth inning, then worked up to a 3–2 count on the next batter. He stepped off the mound, took off his cap, wiped his face with the sleeve of his jersey, then stepped in again.

Crack! A high fly to short left field! Terry sprinted after it. "I'll take it!" he yelled.

"I've got it!" another voice yelled in front of him.

He glanced down for an instant and saw Tony running back toward him. *What shall I do?* he thought. *I can't risk another collision!*

Then he heard Ed yell, "It's Tony's ball! Tony's ball!"

"Take it, Tony!" Terry shouted.

He slowed down and watched Tony catch the ball with little effort.

"Nice catch, Tony," he said, smiling.

A grin flashed over Tony's face. "Thanks, Terry," he said.

Terry trotted back to his position, feeling pretty good that this time the play had worked perfectly. Even Tony had cracked a grin, as if to say, *We did it right this time, didn't we?*

A hot grounder to Jeff resulted in a double play. Three outs.

"Come on, men," Coach Harper snapped. "This is the fifth inning and we're two runs behind. What d'you say?"

Jeff walked. Tony tried twice to bunt him down to second and fouled both times. He then hit a scratch single to short. Jeff ran to second in time to beat the throw. Two on, no outs, and Terry was up.

He glanced at the coach, saw him brush his left hand across his chest.

The bunt signal was on.

12

NERVOUSLY, Terry stepped into the box and waited for the pitch. In it came, knee high. He moved into bunting stance and stuck out his bat.

A neat bunt down the third-base line! The Yellow Jacket third baseman rushed in to field it, scooped it up and whipped it to first. Out! But both Jeff and Tony had advanced a base and were now in good scoring position.

"Nice bunt, Terry," Coach Harper smiled as Terry came trotting in to the dugout.

"Thanks," said Terry.

Rich took a 1–1 count, then singled through short. Both Jeff and Tony scored. 3–3! The Forest Lakers' bench and fans went wild.

Jeff and Tony ran in to the bench, Jeff sitting down beside Terry. He moved over to give Tony room, and Tony sat down. Both boys were breathing hard from their run.

"Nice bunt, man!" Tony laughed, socking Terry playfully on the knee.

"Thanks," said Terry.

"We've got to keep this up," Tony said, turning his attention to the ball game. "We've got to pull ahead of those guys."

"If we pull together we will," Terry said. "But we've got to pull together."

Tony looked at him. Their eyes locked

in heavy silence. Then Tony nodded. "Yeah, you're right. It's the only way."

The rally continued. Bud singled, advancing Rich to third, and Ed stepped to the plate.

"Drive it, Ed!" Terry shouted above the din rising from the fans.

Crack! The ball sailed over short for a single and Rich scored. 4–3! The Forest Lakers' bench emptied. The guys jumped, danced, and cheered, their cries mixing with the triumphant yell exploding from the fans.

"Keep it going, Stu!" Terry yelled. "Get a hit!"

Stu didn't, though. He flied out to left for the second out, and Caesar popped out to short for the third.

"Let's hold 'em!" Tony cried as the team

ran out to the field in the top of the sixth.

The Yellow Jackets' lead-off man laced a pitch between first and second for a double, then scored on a single to center field that drew a terrific applause from the Yellow Jacket rooters. 4–4!

Terry saw Tony grab up a handful of dust and toss it angrily aside.

"Stick in there, Tony!" Terry yelled. "Let's not give up, man!"

Tony looked at him and smiled as he lifted his hand with the V for victory sign. "We'll pull together! Okay?"

"Okay!" cried Terry, and thought, *Was the atmosphere really thawing between him and Tony?* It was hard to tell just yet.

The next Yellow Jacket popped a fly to short. One away.

Woody caught Tony's soft throw, rubbed the ball a minute, then stepped back on the mound. He checked the runner on second, stretched and threw. A solid blow to Rich in center field! He caught the fly and rifled it to third. But the runner, after tagging up at second, slid safely under Ed's outstretched glove.

"Two away!" Tony shouted, waving two fingers at the outfielders. "One more to get!"

The next hitter came to the plate and Terry took a dozen steps in toward the infield. He remembered that the hitter didn't have much power. The guy had knocked two singles, and both were shallow drives over short.

Woody mopped his brow with a handkerchief, stepped on the mound, got his signal from Stu, and pitched. *Crack!* Another solid blow over short!

Even as Terry ran in to field the ball he

saw the runner on third already sprinting for home. He wanted to shout "Tony, come here!," but realized that he didn't have to. Tony was on his way toward him.

Terry pegged him the ball, and in one swift motion Tony whipped it home. Stu caught the ball near the plate and put it on the runner as he slid in under a cloud of dust.

"Out!" shouted the ump.

Three outs! The Forest Lakers' fans thundered their unanimous approval.

Tony waited for Terry to reach him, and both ran off the field together. "Nice play, Terry!" Tony exclaimed. "You played your position perfectly!"

Terry grinned. "He hadn't hit too far before," he said. "I figured he wouldn't hit too far this time either."

"Hey, what a memory!" cried Tony.

"With my kind of arm I need it!" Terry chuckled happily.

"Yeah. I guess I'll just have to run out to left field everytime a ball is hit to you," Tony said, laughing.

The crowd gave Woody a big hand as he stepped to the plate. A moment later they let out a sad "Ah! Too bad, Woody!" as he popped out to short.

Jeff didn't do any better, grounding out to third for the second out.

"Come on, Tony!" Terry cried as Tony stepped to the plate. "Get on!"

Electric silence charged the air as Tony waited for the first pitch to come in. It blazed in chest high and he swung. *Crack!* The ball streaked past the pitcher to the outfield for a single and once again the Forest Lakers' bench clambered out and cheered with gusto.

"Get a hit, Terry!" Tony yelled from first base. "Get a hit!"

Terry felt the sweat on his hands as he gripped the bat and waited for the pitch. It came in, but it was high. *No!* a voice inside him warned. *Don't swing!* He let it go by.

"Ball!" cried the ump.

The next pitch was lower. It grooved the heart of the plate and Terry swung. The blow was solid and sounded like music to Terry's ears. He saw the ball sail like a rocket out to deep right center field. Even as he dropped his bat and bolted to first he heard the victorious cheer erupting from the Forest Lakers' fans. He crossed first, second, and was held up by the coach at third.

Then he saw the fans spilling out of

the stands, and the guys running toward him, led by Tony himself.

"Nice smash, Terry!" Tony cried, pumping his hand. "You won the ball game, man!"

Terry blinked happily. "Like we said . . ."

"I know," Tony interrupted. "We have to pull together. And we did, didn't we?"

Terry nodded.

After the shouting and handshaking were over, Terry and some of the other guys picked up the bases and equipment and put them into the canvas bags for the coach, then headed for home.

"Terry, I — I don't know how to say this," Tony said uneasily, "except that I'm sorry."

"Why? Because I hit that triple?" Terry laughed.

"No. You know what I mean."

Their eyes met for a moment, and Terry nodded silently.

"I'm having a birthday party at my house next Saturday," Tony said. "I'm inviting the whole team. I hope you can make it."

Terry felt a lump lodge in his throat. He had been hoping that Tony would invite him. He grinned and poked his new friend on the shoulder.

"Try and stop me," he said, and turned to see Mick smiling happily at them.

How many of these Matt Christopher sports classics have you read?

- ❑ Baseball Pals
- ❑ The Basket Counts
- ❑ Catch That Pass!
- ❑ Catcher with a Glass Arm
- ❑ Challenge at Second Base
- ❑ The Counterfeit Tackle
- ❑ The Diamond Champs
- ❑ Dirt Bike Racer
- ❑ Dirt Bike Runaway
- ❑ Face-Off
- ❑ Football Fugitive
- ❑ The Fox Steals Home
- ❑ The Great Quarterback Switch
- ❑ Hard Drive to Short
- ❑ The Hockey Machine
- ❑ Ice Magic
- ❑ Johnny Long Legs
- ❑ The Kid Who Only Hit Homers
- ❑ Little Lefty
- ❑ Long Shot for Paul
- ❑ Long Stretch at First Base
- ❑ Look Who's Playing First Base
- ❑ Miracle at the Plate
- ❑ No Arm in Left Field
- ❑ Red-Hot Hightops
- ❑ Return of the Home Run Kid
- ❑ Run, Billy, Run
- ❑ Shortstop from Tokyo
- ❑ Soccer Halfback
- ❑ The Submarine Pitch
- ❑ Supercharged Infield
- ❑ Tackle Without a Team
- ❑ Tight End
- ❑ Too Hot to Handle
- ❑ Touchdown for Tommy
- ❑ Tough to Tackle
- ❑ Wingman on Ice
- ❑ The Year Mom Won the Pennant

All available in paperback from Little, Brown and Company

Join the Matt Christopher Fan Club!

To become an official member of the Matt Christopher Fan Club, send a self-addressed, stamped legal-size envelope to:

Matt Christopher Fan Club
34 Beacon Street
Boston, MA 02108